Dominated By My Neighbours 2

~o~

Reverse Harem Chronicles

Book 9

TIMEA TOKES

ISBN: 9798704123828

DEDICATION

To all my lovely readers out there. Remember, no matter what your dreams are (naughty or not), you have everything you need to make them come true.

If you love my writing style, please check out my other titles on Amazon, and follow me on my blog & website for a FREE pdf copy of Squirm Under My Watch, FREE Audiobooks, and other goodies, to say a personal thank you to you all.

I am also hosting a monthly signed paperback giveaway, with at least 2 winners each month. So, please stay tuned, and share the love that's deep inside all of you.

Thank you!

www.timeatokes.com

ACKNOWLEDGMENTS

All characters and events in these stories are purely fictional, therefore any resemblance to real people (living or dead) or events is a coincidence.

All characters would be at least 18 years of age, too, should they be real.

Caution: Contains descriptive sex scenes and adult contents.

Intended for a mature audience of at least 18+ (or more, depending on your country of residence and the local law).

Chapter 1

~o~

I pull into the parking lot, hands trembling on the steering wheel. I have exactly ten minutes to spare, two minutes more than I need. I hate being late, but today I'm surprised I'm even here. I wanted to bail out so badly, but I also knew that Sophie would find me regardless. It isn't too difficult when you live next door.

What I couldn't possibly have figured out is the fact that I'm also living next door to a super-secret sex-book-club where just about anything goes. My eyes mist over at the memory, and a blush creeps up my cheek, my pulse skyrocketing as the image manifests in my mind's eye. Sophie being spread out and taken by not only her husband, but that other guy.

What was his name again?

I silently curse at the lamp post I almost hit, as if my clumsiness and distracted state was its fault. And in some ways, it is. I shouldn't be here. Not after what happened last week, and not since what I'm planning to do later on today. How could I face all these women who keep mocking me? But more importantly, how can I face the one that doesn't?

With a sigh I check my reflection in the rear-view mirror, frowning at the pink lipstick and the mascara. I have no idea what I was thinking. I don't even wear makeup for weddings, and now this. My life has been turned upside down since that ominous book club and I know there is no going back.

But the most frustrating part isn't even what I witnessed. I have watched porn before, so I'm not prude when it comes to watching others have sex. My confusion lies in my own feelings and desires the whole evening evoked. They now don't let me

1

sleep, eat, or practically exist. I am a prisoner of my own twisted mind, and it just gets more confusing by the minute.

I'm too scared to ask about the handsome dark stranger that instructed me to masturbate in front of him, nor am I willing to accept how watching Sophie herself made me feel. Something more stirred within me than mere desire to be taken the way she had been, but I'm trying to avoid the subject.

Right, I either need to get out and make a run for it, or stay in the car and hide underneath a bridge for the next... Yeah, well, for ever. Or until I can sell my house. With a swift shake of my head, I grab my gym bag and slam the car door shut behind me. A familiar voice I've been dreading all week greets me cautiously:

'Hello, Alice. Long time no see.'

Is that accusation in her voice? Hard to tell. With a deep breath and my heart in my throat I spin around and fake a smile at her.

'Hi, Sophie. Tell me about it! It felt like for ever, right?'

I let out a nervous laugh, running a hand through my brunette braid. She raises an eyebrow, but her smile fails to reach her eyes. Her usual cheerfulness is missing, too.

'Right.'

Her eyes search my face, then the tiniest smile creeps onto her scrumptious lips, making my heart beat even faster. I can't help but feel like I have been caught, although I'm not sure what I did.

'So, are you ready for today?'

For a moment I'm not sure whether she is referring to yoga class or the book club, so I simply shrug, trying to brush it off as if it wasn't affecting me the way it did. I don't think she buys it, because her smile is getting wider now.

She leisurely walks over and I take a step back, my back flush against the coldness of my car. Sophie runs a finger down my cheek, cocking her head to the side. Her raven curls bounce around her milky shoulders, the once pleasant strawberry scent making me want to gag right now.

'I can see you are more prepared than last time. Does that mean you are ready to participate?'

There.

She hasn't even asked me what I thought about last time or whether I was okay with it all. She could have assumed that I'm still here because I don't want to break a habit, and not because I'm willing to participate in her sex-book-club. But judging by the amused expression on her beautiful face, she knows the truth. I gulp my fear down and shrug again.

'Watching is fun enough, I guess.'

Her laughter sends a shiver down my spine.

'Yes, your admirer certainly agrees with you on that. Me, personally... Well, I like a bit of both...'

What's with the innuendos today?

I smile at her weakly, then nod, feeling bold and brave all of a sudden.

'I see. Well, maybe I will try it one day. So... which book are we reading this week?'

I don't even mention that I think the reading material should be discussed upfront, so people could *actually* read it, but I guess I need to learn that in Sophie's world, nothing is what it looks like. She picks the end of my braid up, caressing my neck with the tip. I shudder.

'Ah, you know, it's supposed to be the second part of *Taken during the Storm*. This part is about the main character being robbed in her kitchen, but of course, nothing truly forced. It's just for the show.'

She trails off, drawing circles with the tip of my braid, raising goosebumps on my skin. I nod, biting my lower lip, even though the plot doesn't really make sense. I feel like somehow I got transported into a really weird porn movie (or a nightmare, I'm not sure yet).

But then if this is so bad, then why am I so curious still?

'Sure. Are you playing again?'

For some reason, the prospect of watching Sophie again sends a thrill down my spine, and when she shakes her head, my heart sinks. I keep telling myself that it's only because I like imagining myself in her place, and that the real thing would be too much for now.

'Nah... I want to be the one to watch this time. That's why I was hoping you were going to say you are ready to play.'

My eyebrows shoot up, her words bringing me out of my stupor.

'Me? Why me?'

She shrugs, her black hair oozing its fresh strawberry scent.

'I told you I like you. I meant it.'

With heart hammering like crazy in my chest, I can hardly hear her words, although their meaning finally sinks in. I have no idea what I'm saying or doing, only the fact that I'm doing it registers in my brain (and only when it's too late):

'In that case, well... Maybe if I knew who the guys were...'

I did expect a vehement reaction from Sophie, but I didn't expect her to jump into my neck, knocking me back against my car, the cold seeping into my back, hardening my nipples under the gym top.

'You see, I knew you were going to be a perfect addition to our little club.'

I clear my throat, embarrassed, and she pulls away, her cheeks flushed.

'Right, I'm sorry, Alice, it's just been such a long time since we had someone else on the podium, I guess I lost my manners.'

I nod at her weakly, all blood draining from my own face.

Christ, what have I just agreed to?

'So... about the guys...'

My voice is shaking, but she doesn't seem to notice. She facepalms herself, shaking her head, the raven curls following her every movement.

'I'm sorry again. Chris will definitely be one of them, especially if *you* are playing, but I'm not sure about the other one just yet.'

I furrow my brows at her.

'Um, Chris?'

Her smile widens as she grabs my hand, pulling me after her. I almost drop my car keys and the gym bag. I steal one last glance at the comfort of my car, then leave it behind, along with my sanity. That could be the only explanation for me wanting to do this: I lost my mind.

'Yeah, the guy who watched you last time. Don't tell me you already forgot...'

The joke doesn't sound funny, and the knot in my stomach twitches. Still, recalling his cheeky smile and those eyes that were ready to devour me sends my pulse racing.

'I never forget anything.'

I whisper, half-hoping that Sophie doesn't hear it. But I'm not that lucky. She glances back over her shoulder as we reach the entrance to the gym, the gleam in her eyes matching the heat with which Chris looked at me last week.

'Good. But remember, some things need to be lived first before you can store them in your memory.'

I gulp again, watching her hips sway as she leads me up the stairs, her black yoga pants doing nothing to hide her muscle-clad curves. The wind picks up again outside, reaching me through an open window. My nipples harden and my breath hitches, but it's only partly because of the sudden difference in the temperature.

I'm in bigger trouble than I thought I could ever be...

~o~

Chapter 2

~o~

I t's funny how there is always something bigger to be afraid of than your previous fears, rendering them small and meaningless. While I was terrified of facing the class before, now nobody pays me any attention, except for Sophie, of course. She tries to chat to me about what's going to happen in the evening, but it's all a blur, really. I don't understand half of the words anyway.

At least I guess anger and fear makes me more flexible, which is a good thing, earning my very first compliment from the teacher. Under different circumstances, I would be over the moon, but I hardly remember doing the pose in the first place.

Time becomes irrelevant, and I soon find myself in Sophie's room, blinking like an idiot or someone with a mental illness, wondering how I got there. For a moment I debate whether I truly am dreaming, because all the details are quite hazy, but I guess if you are so focused on something, your autopilot kicks in.

'Right, so we need to get you into the right clothes. Have you got ready down there?'

My eyes shift to hers, but the expression must be blank in them, because she lets out a sigh, shaking her raven curls. She sits down next to me on the bed, covering my hand with hers.

'Listen, Alice, you know you don't have to do this, right? I mean, you only watched us once, if you are not up to it, I understand.'

I shake my head, even though fear is gripping at my heart. I'm not even sure why I want to prove myself, or who to. Sophie? Chris? Myself? Probably all, not necessarily in that order.

'No, I'm fine, I just don't get why I need to be so prepared when it's only for show and nobody really sees all the details anyway.'

I bite my lower lip, the weight slightly lifting off my shoulder. Sophie smiles at me, running a hand down my cheek, making me shudder.

'Sweetheart... People can *sense* how ready you are, even if they can't see everything. You are feeding their fantasies and their imagination, but that's not what it's about. Not really.'

I raise an eyebrow at her, watching in shock and horror as she peels my tank top off, revealing my naked breasts. She looks at them for a long moment, then goes on to remove my yoga pants, too. I forget to object.

'So... what is it about then?'

I ask, curiosity taking over. She pulls my knickers off, and I don't think I ever felt so exposed and vulnerable in my entire life. Or aroused, even though I have no idea why. Sophie pats my neatly trimmed pubic hair, sending a shiver down my spine. While she replies, her eyes are still on my pussy.

'Your own pleasure and fantasies, of course. Look, every week we try to choose a topic that's taboo, but one that most women and men fantasize about.'

She trails off, her hands pushing my legs apart. I automatically lean back on the bed, blushing.

'Um, what are you doing?'

She lets out a laugh, opening the top drawer on her bedside cabinet.

'What do you think, silly?'

Because I don't reply, she shakes her head again, a cheeky smile on her lips.

'I don't know if you remember, because your eyes were all glazed over till like a minute ago, but once on stage, you won't have much time to get wet for the guys that fuck you.'

The harsh and crude words fall of her tongue naturally, yet hearing them feels so unnatural. She pulls out two items from the drawer, and my eyes go wide. Before I could say anything though, she closes her palms around them, caressing the devices.

'I always say that it's better to be prepared, especially when you have to act out a scenario where you don't really want to have sex. You will be robbed, remember?'

I nod meekly, watching as she pours some lube onto both ends of the double dildo. I clear my throat.

'I thought I was only going to be... you know...'

She raises an eyebrow at me, placing the double dildo at both my entrances.

'No, I don't. And spread your legs wider for me. Slide a bit further down, too.'

I don't know why, but I automatically obey, cursing silently because she is going to make me say it. Clearing my throat, I blurt it out as fast as I can:

'Fine. I thought I was only going to be fucked in my pussy, not in both holes.'

The words leave me breathless and Sophie laughs.

'You aren't the adventurous type, are you?'

I open my mouth to reply, but she pushes the dildos an inch into both of my holes and I gasp. The one that's supposed to go into my pussy slides in easily, considering that I'm already dripping wet, but the one in my ass doesn't move. Sophie frowns, then pulls them out completely.

'Have you had anal sex before?'

She asks, her face turning serious. I shake my head, blushing some more. Her eyebrows shoot up and she runs a hand through her raven curls.

'Ah, I see. Well, I can inform the guys, and of course, they won't do anything you don't want. I assume you don't want it?'

Once again, I hesitate, and Sophie nods, placing her hand on my pubic hair. She draws tentative circles around my clit, as if deep in thought.

'I get that. You want it, but you are scared.'

She looks away, clicking her tongue, then pulls out a small butt plug from the drawer, then turns back to me.

'I tell you what then. I am going to get you ready for tonight, and there won't be any funny business, okay? But I will also ease you into the butt-game. Deal?'

I bite my lower lip again and Sophie frowns, so I nod quickly.

'Deal.'

I breathe, and she looks at my lips in a weird way for a second, then her eyes return to my pussy. She licks her lips, and another shudder runs through me.

'Right, back to the task at hand. Hope you are ready.'

I'm not, but I'm not going to let her know that just yet…

~o~

Chapter 3

~o~

Sophie produces a vibrator this time, similar in size to what I'm used to, except for one thing: I have never had another woman pleasure me before. And although I know she only wants to get me ready for the guys, it still feels weird and awkward.

'Just relax and think of this as practice for later. After all, you won't always be pleasured by guys only.'

I gulp, watching her hands push my knees apart.

'I won't?'

My voice is as shaky as my body, and Sophie pats my inner thigh, making me jump. She rolls her eyes at me, pushing the 'on' button on the vibrator. The gentle buzz raises goosebumps on my arms, making the tiny hairs stand at the nape of my neck.

'Of course not. I like to think that my book club is quite open-minded when it comes to these things.'

Yeah, no shit Sherlock...

I let out a sigh, looking away. I honestly don't know how I feel about this. Sophie must notice, too, because the vibrator stops halfway towards my pussy.

'Is there something wrong? You can tell me, you know...'

I let out another sigh. I want to talk to her about all my frustrations and insecurities, and the pressure within my heart is so strong I can't take it anymore. If I do this, then I need her to know.

'It's just...'

I begin, but my voice trembles. Sophie smiles at me reassuringly, her blue eyes gentle and caring. She even props herself on one elbow next to me, our eyes level this time. Just like a girl's night I never had – although I don't assume teenagers do this sort of stuff during sleepovers.

'Go on, it's just the two of us.'

Sophie says, unaware that's one of the things I'm scared of. I clear my throat, attempting the impossible once again:

'Well, it's just that a week ago I didn't even know that your sex-book-club existed, and now I'm going to be on the podium, being taken by two guys I don't know.'

I take a deep breath, and she shrugs.

'Would it help if I asked Steve to be one of them?'

I shake my head, blushing.

'No, that's not really the point. Not knowing the guys is the least of my concerns.'

She hums, tucking a stray strand of brown hair behind my ear. I am momentarily distracted by her gentleness, but her next question quickly snaps me out of it:

'So, what is?'

I look away, silent for a long time. Sophie doesn't pressure me or rush me. I truly feel like she understands. She must have felt insecure about one thing or another. Nobody is perfect. When the silence is too painful to bare, a sob escapes me, and I speak before I could change my mind:

'I'm worried that people won't like me. I mean, what's there to like?'

I don't expect an answer, I really don't. Anytime I said the same thing, I got apologetic shrugs, or people telling me that I'm beautiful on the inside, which always confirmed my deepest fears. But Sophie surprises me by placing a finger under my chin, turning my face back towards her. The storm behind her beautiful blue irises makes me gasp.

'You are such a stupid woman.'

She says in an angry voice, gripping my chin firmly. My lips wobble, because at least I thought she wouldn't insult me any further. I want to look away, but her hand and her eyes hold me captive. She suddenly runs a finger along the line of my lower lip, leaning close. Her voice is barely a whisper now.

'You are the most beautiful creature I've ever seen.'

My eyes go wide at her confession, but before I could react, her lips capture mine in a searing kiss. Another gasp escapes me, and I automatically put my hands onto her shoulders. It's like I have been starving for all eternity, only realising it when a drop of water touched my lips. If it wasn't for the kiss, I would have died without knowing.

Sophie's lips are soft, yet her kiss is possessive and demanding, her tongue invading my mouth. All I can do is return her passion, while my whole body is shaking with a never-before-known desire that's stronger than anything I have ever experienced. I don't even know what I'm craving, but I do know that if I don't get it soon, I will go crazy.

She is pushing me into the mattress, and my legs buckle from its intensity. I've never known such passion could exist, especially not between... She suddenly breaks the kiss, her velvety lips brushing over mine one last time, and the lack of contact leaves me breathless.

Neither of us speaks for a while, only our ragged breathing fills the room. There is a knock on the door, and before either of us could react, Steve pops his head in. He doesn't even batter an eye at my nakedness. In fact, he completely ignores me, addressing his wife:

'I hope you guys are ready. The audience is growing a bit impatient.'

There is no accusation in his tone, and yet I feel like I just did something I shouldn't have and I have been caught doing it. Fair enough, I am laying next to his wife and I'm naked, so there isn't much left to the imagination. Sophie suddenly looks at me, then shakes her head, turning back towards Steve.

'Alice needs more time. I will take her place.'

Steve lets out a sigh.

'People won't be happy. I think they are bored of watching the same show over and over, if you know what I mean.'

Sophie gets up, discarding her clothes within a second. My eyes go wide at her gorgeous body, and my lips tingle from the kiss we shared. I close my legs, painfully aware of my own nakedness.

Without looking back at us, Sophie walks up to her wardrobe and picks out an outfit similar to last time. Then, pausing for a moment, throws a gown at me, too.

'Put that on. Chris will be waiting for you where you were sitting last time. You might as well enjoy the show if you are here.'

Then, turning to Steve:

'Darling, you know I can make sure they get their money's worth.'

He looks at her for a long moment, then grins as widely as his face would allow.

'Oh, I know better than anyone.'

Sophie smiles at him, turning her back towards him, so he can do the hidden zipper up, the one that runs alongside her spine. The gown itself is see-through, an emerald green muslin dress that leaves nothing to the imagination. Her blue eyes suddenly spot me gawking and I blush once again. She cocks her head to the side.

'Don't feel bad about what happened. Think about it as a taster. We will get you ready next time, okay?'

I squirm and she laughs.

'Come on, you need to get dressed. You don't want Chris to see you completely naked yet.'

She walks up to me, and I let her slide the golden material over my head. The bottom hem barely covers my thigh. Sophie leans close, whispering into my ear:

'Leave your knickers up here. I have a feeling that you won't need them tonight.'

And with that, she grabs my hand once again and we follow Steve out of the room, the scent of strawberries reminding me of the sweetness of Sophie's lips. I know it's not nice and it isn't going to happen, but for a moment, my mind wanders onto dangerous waters, imagining what would have happened if Steve didn't walk in when he did.

~o~

Chapter 4

~o~

'm only half surprised when I find Chris sitting in the chair that was previously mine. I'm not even sure I have the right to protest, but Sophie pulls me back last minute, tucking my hair behind my ear before whispering:

'He is quite alright, isn't he?'

She even licks her lips while glancing at him. Seeing my frown, she laughs, gently pinching my arm.

'Don't worry, I will leave him for you. I'm not greedy like that.'

I inhale sharply.

'That's not what I...'

'Hello gorgeous!'

Chris' voice beams from behind me, sending a shiver down my spine. Sophie winks at me before disappearing behind the thick curtains, getting ready for the show. With heart pounding so hard and fast I'm sure everyone around me can hear it, I slowly turn around, my dress making a swishing sound. I rub the spot Sophie touched, more for comfort than anything else.

'Well, aren't you going to sit down?'

He asks, head cocked to the side, a wicked grin on his handsome face. I look into those grey eyes of his, now covered by a red mask. I gulp, looking around.

'There don't seem to be any spare seats left.'

I mumble, embarrassed and aroused at the same time, the mental imprint of Sophie's fingers never leaving me. It was sinful, hot, and something I never thought I would do. And yet, because nobody knows, it kind of thrills me that I share this secret now with her. Chris shakes his head, patting his knee.

'There is plenty of room here. Come, I won't bite. Unless you want me to, of course...'

I shudder as his words sink in, and take a step backwards. Chris laughs so wholeheartedly that it pisses me off. Why is he making fun of me all of a sudden? Sure, I'm not adventurous, but all this is wrong anyway...

'Relax, I won't fuck you tonight.'

His harsh words should scare me. They really should. They should also encourage me to get the hell out of here. And yet here I am, dripping at the thought of him having his way with me, a pang of disappointment building in my gut because he won't.

What's wrong with me?

The curtain is pulled, and the lights are dimmed. I look around once again, but nobody is watching. With a deep sigh, I step closer, and before I know it, I'm sitting on Chris' lap, facing the podium. His closeness is even more arousing than him watching me last week. When he shifts, so he can whisper in my ear, I feel his massive erection press into my butt.

Has he been playing with himself?

The thought sends another shiver down my spine, and an unearthly desire to watch him do that overwhelms me.

'That's a good girl.'

He whispers, making the soft hairs at the nape of my neck stand to attention. Then, adding in a clipped tone:

'I wanted to be up there with you tonight. But I will honour your request – for now. But trust me, you won't want to deny me for ever.'

I gulp, nodding, just in time as Sophie appears on stage, hair wet from a shower. She is barely covered by a towel, her shapely legs and the swell of her breasts clearly visible. Droplets of water travel down her slender body, and I feel my own nipples harden while I'm watching her. I let out a soft moan, recalling our kiss, my knees automatically pressing closer together. Chris chuckles, the vibrations making me shudder.

'Well, well. You are a bit of a dark horse then. I like it.'

I want to argue with him, but the words get caught in my throat. Could it really be? All those unwelcome thoughts and desires, all those dreams since last week... I did enjoy watching

Sophie, but that kiss and what she did put things into a new perspective. And although I can't put my finger on what I'm feeling right now, it's definitely not innocent.

'Who's there?'

Sophie asks, suddenly looking around in alarm. Instead of the kitchen, the podium hosts a four-poster bed with massive wooden poles in each corner, holding up a canopy of muslin. The transparent material gently moves, as if there was air coming from somewhere. Sophie laughs nervously.

'Ah, I must have left a window open. Silly me.'

She turns around, having her back to the bed, and walks up to a tiny window, closing it. Two things happen. Number one: her towel falls onto the floor, revealing her shapely ass to the whistling audience. Number two: two masked men jump out from underneath the bed. I let out a gasp, wanting to warn Sophie. I can feel Chris' arms tighten around me.

'Relax, it's just for the show. Apparently, this fantasy ranked second highest among the group.'

Sophie shrieks when she sees the two men, and I relax a bit when I realise that one of them is her husband once again, and the other one is their third wheel from last week. All is good then, I guess.

I glance back at Chris, and his grin widens, the red mask accentuating the silver glint in his expressive eyes. Right now they are telling me he would do anything to be able to do things to me. Things I would probably regret. I can smell the champagne on his hot breath, and I can feel his heartbeat. It should feel scary to be so close to someone I barely know.

So, why am I so turned on right now?

'I guess it is yours as well then?'

I ask as calmly as I can. If I seriously consider having sex with this guy (which I haven't decided yet), then I need to know what his intentions are. I mean, I know this is basically a sex-book-club, so I don't have high hopes, but still. I didn't sign up for weird fetishes. I release a shaky breath as he shakes his head.

'No. I prefer my partner to be a willing and eager participant.'

I turn back towards Sophie, who is now struggling against her restraints now, a ballgag in her mouth. Steve throws her onto the bed, then goes onto tying her arms up, while Pete does the same with her ankles. Sophie is spread out, and once the two men stand next to her, their erect cocks in their fists, she stops wriggling. A shudder runs through me as Steve removes her ballgag.

'You know the score. If you use that pretty mouth of yours for anything other than sucking, we will need to punish you.'

Steve's voice is husky, and there are a few catcalls from the crowd. Sophie looks down at Steve's cock, then back up at him defiantly.

'I thought you wanted me to scream, so you know you are doing a great job.'

Steve doesn't answer, but shoves his cock between Sophie's still parted lips.

'Oh, you will scream plenty. But first, you will give us what we came here for. Pete, teach her a lesson.'

Pete nods then kneels onto the bed, between Sophie's thighs. She starts struggling against her ties, while Steve fucks her mouth so fast that it's hard to keep track. She occasionally even makes a gagging sound, and my own mouth goes dry when I think that I would have been up there instead of her. She practically saved me from this.

As if reading my mind, Chris whispers into my ear:

'Next week will be my own fantasy, just so you know. Would you like to know what it is?'

I focus on his words too much, realising too late that his hand slid down my dress, and is now lifting the hem up. The fact that I'm not wearing any panties comes to mind, and my pulse quickens. Interesting enough though, the idea of stopping him doesn't even cross my mind.

'Only because I don't like surprises.'

I mumble, my voice shaky. Chris laughs, and I watch as Pete pushes his cock deep inside Sophie's butt. She cries out in pain, but Steve's cock muffles the sound. Someone cheers in the background, and I notice that people are moaning all around me now. It's as if I have been sitting in a bubble, and now it's popped. Everything is so loud, so intense, so... arousing. I can't take it anymore.

'I'm sure I can change that later. But very well then. I will tell you after the show. You disappeared too quickly last time, you naughty woman.'

I want to correct him, because it was *him* who disappeared, but his fingers find my clit and instead of a protest, a loud moan escapes me. He chuckles again, pulling me firmly against his muscular body.

'Yes, that's right. Don't hold back. I want to hear you moan.'

Of course, I do the opposite: biting the inside of my cheek, I hold my breath and stay as quiet as I can. He pinches my clit, and I stifle a shriek of my own.

'Have it your way then.'

And with that, he covers my mouth with his other hand, while he inserts two fingers inside my dripping pussy, his thumb pressing down on my sensitive clit. My eyes search for Sophie, but she is still busy sucking Steve off, while Pete is pounding away in her ass. All I can do is give in to the desire building up deep inside me.

'I so want to fuck you right now. I want to take you in any way and every way I can.'

I let out a sigh as his fingers curl against my G-spot, and I lean into him. I almost tell him to do it then, but then he adds a bit more soberly, his fingers halting:

'But I won't. Not until you are ready to experience it in front of the others. Being watched adds so much to the pleasure. You will see. But until then...'

Resuming his gentle teasing, he finger-fucks me until I can't hold it back anymore. I scream against his palm, the orgasm temporarily blinding me. I don't mind though. Closing my eyes, I listen to all the moans and groans that fill the room, mine included this time.

I'm still panting when he pulls his fingers out of my pussy, and I don't object when he brings them up to my lips. I even dart my tongue out, first licking the length of his fingers, then sucking on them, as if I was sucking on his cock. I have no idea why, but something snapped in me once again, and my inhibitions are gone.

But then again, he just provided me with an awesome O, so I guess it's understandable.

I glance back at the podium, but Sophie hasn't finished yet. I know I will regret this, but I suddenly turn towards Chris, fully aware that he is still rock hard for me.

'How about we act out your fantasy now, instead of you just telling me?'

He raises a dark eyebrow, making his eyes look extremely sexy under the red mask.

'But I haven't even told you what it is yet. I thought you weren't ready, and you didn't like surprises.'

I shrug, turning back towards the scene. A shiver runs through me as I watch Sophie's dark curls bounce around as she bobs her head up and down on Steve's shaft.

'As you said, I don't want to deny you for ever.'

Then, glancing back at him over my shoulder:

'Unless you changed your mind already?'

I hope he sees the challenge in my green eyes, and when his own pair lights up, I know I'm winning. What, I'm not sure yet, but I also know that whatever he is offering, I want in.

'Ladies first. Unless you want us to start here.'

To show me what he means, he shifts his hips, so that his hard cock presses against my butt again. I nod, getting up and holding out a hand.

'I'm sure the audience won't mind.'

He nods at me, a small smile on his lips:

'They will be thrilled. And so will I.'

I smile at him, taking in his gorgeous features for a long moment. But if I'm honest with myself, he isn't even the one I'm looking forward to having the most. Deep, deep inside, I think I want to fuck Sophie...

~o~

~o~

Dominated By My Neighbours 3, Book 10 in the Reverse Harem Chronicles is coming soon.

Please visit my website (www.timeatokes.com) to sign up for my newsletter, and I would really appreciate it if you let me know what you thought about this short story.

Thanks a lot!

~o~

A tempting taste of other, bite-size erotica, from the naughty pen of Timea Tokes:

~o~

A SPECIAL CUP OF COFFEE
(SAMPLE)

Don't worry, this is a first for me, too..."
Ah, is that supposed to comfort me?
Very promising.

I try to pull on the restraints, but he has tied me up tightly. My heart is pounding, and I can't see a thing because of the blindfold. All I can do is wait helplessly until he figures out his next move, wondering how could I have gotten myself into this mess.

A mere hour ago I was sitting at the bar, minding my own business, drinking heavily, as if there was no tomorrow. Right up to the moment when the bartender offered to make me a special cup of coffee. Which I'm still waiting for, by the way.

Just saying.

Okay, I wasn't that naïve to think that we would actually be drinking coffee, cuddling on his couch, no. And as I said, I didn't want that anyway. I wanted hot, steamy, and kinky sex. And although he hasn't touched me yet, not in that way anyway, this whole situation is kinky alright.

"Just try to relax and clear your mind..."

He is really getting into this. Does he have a guidebook that he is citing from? I must admit that hearing his voice alone makes me shiver all over. It is sexy as hell, and I can already feel the previous dampness of my thong worsening by the minute. I wonder how long is he going to keep me suspended like this? It's funny how you lose all of your senses when you can't see.

No kidding!

Although I can hear his voice, but only when he allows me to, and I still can't tell where it's coming from. For all I know he could be standing in the doorway, ready to lock me in, leaving me to suffer for God knows how long. I sure as hell hope he isn't planning to make that special cup of coffee *right now.*

But judging by what he just said, I guess I need to do the opposite. In fact, my mind is the only thing that's working perfectly well right now. And my survival instincts, of course. I begin to regret that I didn't listen to my friends. I should have waited for this kind of kink until I knew the guy, let alone trusted him.

Oh my God, I don't even know his name!

"You might feel a little bit cold. Try not to wiggle too much, okay?"

Okay, I was wrong. All my nerves are on edge, and I want to scream from the ice-cold sensation that's burning my left nipple right now.

Little bit cold?

Whatever he put on me makes me want to swear and scream, except I can't. All I can give out is a tiny whimper through my gritted teeth. I want to tell him to stop, to let me go, feeling embarrassed and exposed all of a sudden.

But as quickly as the thought forms in the back of my mind, it evaporates just as quickly when he takes my erect nipple into his mouth. His hot, wet tongue is a relief from the ice-cold sensation, and yet it feels a tad bit more painful, maybe because I am more sensitive than I ever was. He bites down gently, and I can feel the coldness on my right nipple, while he is stroking my left one with his tongue.

I gasp, getting lost in the mixed sensations of hot and cold, pain and pleasure. But it doesn't last long, and as much as I wanted him to stop at first, now I wish that he would continue the sweet torture. An involuntary moan leaves my lips, and he lets out a small chuckle.

"Don't worry, I have only just started."

His words send a jolt of electricity right down to my lady parts, and I'm sure I blush a little, too. I think about my black strapless dress, the black lace push-up bra and the black high heels scattered around the room. I'm not even sure he is wearing anything right now, as after a few passionate kisses, he moved straight onto the subject. He promised it to be fun, erotic and orgasmic.

The last part convinced me, and I'm more and more sure that he is a man who keeps his promises…

~o~

Kiss & Tell Tail
Reverse Harem Fairy Tales
1
Timea Tokes

Three
Policemen
&
Me
Reverse Harem
Chronicles
3
Timea Tokes

<u>**Other Books by Timea Tokes:**</u>

<u>**Reverse Harem Chronicles:**</u>
Three Firemen & Me 1-2
Three Policemen & Me 1-2
Three Billionaires & Me 1-3
Dominated By My Neighbours **(NEW)**

<u>**Reverse Harem Fairy Tales:**</u>
Kiss & Tell Tail 1-5
Snow White Desire **(NEW)**

<u>**BDSM Billionaire:**</u>
Watched **(NEW)**

<u>**Holiday Romance:**</u>
Screwing Miss Scrooge
Mistletoe Boss
Dating The Author (Why Choose)
My Hitch-Hiking Valentine
The Bucket List 1-2
Truth or Dare?
Dominating Magic 1-3

<u>**Other BDSM Romance:**</u>
A Special Cup of Coffee – Pain and Pleasure
Stuck & Shared
Squirm Under My Watch
How About the Rooftop?
Don't Make A Sound
Seducing the Plumber 1-2
Dominating The Escort 1-3
The Good Neighbor 1-5
Forgotten
Blue Highlights

<u>Gay:</u>
The Stranger

<u>Paranormal Romance:</u>
Her First And Last Secret Admirer

<u>Collections of Short Stories:</u>
Claim Me This Winter **(NEW)**
Love Me This Year **(NEW)**

Dominated By Billionaires **(NEW)**
Dominated by Strangers 1
Dominated by Strangers 2
Dominated by Men in Uniforms
Dominating the Escort
Dominating Magic 1-3
Kiss and Tell Tail 1-5

You Had Me At Kinky
You Had Me At Steamy
You Had Me At Rough

Coming Soon:

Dominated By My Neighbours 3 (2021)
Caught (BDSM Billionaire 2) (2021)
Snow White Desire (2021)
A Cupid Mistake (2021)
Hell's Bride (2021)

Follow Timea Tokes on:

Amazon @timea_tokes

Twitter @timea_tokes

Facebook @herfirstsecret

Goodreads @timea_tokes

Sign up to her newsletter, and have a look at her blog for more bite-size erotica, paranormal romance, reviews and more:

www.timeatokes.com

Note from the Author, Timea Tokes:

~o~

My dear, lovely Reader, thank you for taking the time to read my story! I really hope you enjoyed it as much as I did writing it. As always, your feedback is highly valued and much appreciated.

Please do take the time to scroll to the end of the book and leave a review. It would mean the World to me!

And remember, this story is all about your pleasure.

On the next page, you can learn a bit more about me and why I write, but you will also find author interviews (and much more) on my website.

~o~

ABOUT THE AUTHOR

~o~

I have been writing short stories and poems since a young age, but my ultimate goal was creating a novel. Or a series, rather. Now, with my four paranormal romance novels published, as well as more than 30 erotica titles under my belt, , I think I can say that it came true - but this only fuels my desire to write more. After all, we are allowed to dream the same dream (over and over again) - and that's exactly what I'm planning to do :)

I enjoy helping people in any way possible, and I really hope that my books will prove to be inspirational in a way. Whether readers are looking for a swift (and steamy) erotic story, or a paranormal romance, I want them to associate themselves with my characters and realize stuff about themselves in the process.

Yes, even the bad things. Because, in life, there is no black and white, only colors. Therefore, I don't think any of my characters are either good or bad, but rather a little bit of both.

Aren't we all?

Well, if you never had guilty thoughts, never had any self-confidence issues, or if you never wanted something (or someone) who belonged to someone else, then probably my books won't be for you. But, who knows, I might be able to show you a different perspective. I like to experiment with different genres, and new concepts and ideas.

I really enjoy learning as much as I can about people, what makes them tick (and live, laugh, cry, and sigh). In fact, I think our World (and those beyond) are so diverse, ten thousand lifetimes wouldn't be enough to explore it all. But one thing I truly believe in: those who belong in your life will find a way there. Therefore my stories are usually based on chance encounters and ordinary events that take an unexpected turn.

Like a blind date on Valentine's day, or a haircut, or a new job. Who says you can't meet someone 'accidentally'; while going to the hairdresser, someone you lost contact with 500 years ago? Trust me, you can. You just need to brace every day (and every book) with open eyes - and an open heart.

Just remember: my stories are all about you, and you alone. If they capture your attention (and your heart), then I've done my 'job'. I regularly try to release new content, both on Amazon and my blog. Please feel free to have a look, and sign up to my newsletter.

And, just so you know: I care about your opinion, very much so. Whether you liked my work or you didn't, I would be honored if you let me know what it meant for you. It would mean the world to me!

~o~

1. *When did you create your first erotica story, and what was it about?*

Well, my first story wasn't fully erotica, more a romance story. In fact, I never thought that one day I would write anything steamy. Not at all. I was shy, and grew up in an environment, where everything was taboo. Sharing my views on sex with anyone, let alone write about it? No way...

And yet, I soon had to realize that writing romantic stories couldn't happen without the couple getting it on eventually. Especially because the first four books series I created was about the same characters, and they are 100 pages each (which is a lot to go without including a sex scene every now and again). I must admit, I delayed the inevitable for as long as I could, just to realize later how much I enjoyed writing about sex.

Although my first attempts were very timid indeed, I tried to avoid being too explicit or descriptive. I concentrated on the romantic and paranormal aspect of it (the main characters dream about each other, and somehow when I was writing about the dreams, they gave me courage to be a bit braver).

But it wasn't until I started writing my erotic short stories in 2015, when I started to experiment. Well, if you have a look at 'The Good Neighbour', you can see how my explicitness and mood changed throughout the series.

I think I can say that this was the very first fully erotic story I created, fulfilling one of my secret fantasies (no, I don't have a hot neighbour, or at least I don't think I have, but the idea always fascinated me).

2. What (or who) inspired you to start writing erotica?

My own lack of courage, if I'm honest. All my friends were so open about their relationships and their fantasies, so I thought:

"Why do I have to be this way, when I want to explore everything that's out there?"

And as I have always enjoyed writing, I decided to try it out on paper. It started as a therapy I prescribed for myself, and then it escalated, taking me to places I never thought I would visit. I must say that I'm really glad I gave in to temptation.

3. What do you find most challenging when writing these stories?

To let them go when I finish writing them. I believe that it isn't possible, especially when I create a longer story. The characters, the feelings stay with me long after, as they become part of me for at least a little while.

Another aspect of it is that I keep thinking about what others read into them, and whether they convey their meaning in a way that I intended them to. But, just like when you give birth to a child, when writing a story as well you need to give it space after some time.

I once read a quotation (not sure where, or who said it, but it made me smile and I could definitely relate):

"I met the man of my dreams last night.. in chapter five…" *Sigh*

4. Do you write in other genres, and if yes, then would you consider mixing them with erotica?

Yes, and not sure. I ghost-write for a living, as well as create my own stories, which include romance, horror, thriller, fantasy, crime and more, but I'm not sure it would feel right to mix them with erotica. Mind that, I have had some strange requests that were a mixture, like fetish-horror, but it didn't actually include erotica. I suppose it could have, as it was about a foot fetish, which seems to be quite popular. Oh well, another thing to look at in the future :)

My favourite ones are psychological thrillers though, so I could probably turn one of those into erotica, but at the moment I'm thinking of a transition, rather than a mix. So, for example it would start as a thriller, but have a sexual ending. Hmm…

5. Have you written any stories that were inspired by real life events?

Yes. In fact, my very first story, 'Her First and Last Secret Admirer' (the four books I mentioned earlier) started with an actual recurring medieval dream, which I then implemented into the plot, creating a story and background for it. If it wasn't for that urge to put the whole thing into writing, I probably would never have picked up the courage to write at all. Now it is both in print and on Kindle, so I guess it was a nice bargain :)

I think that writing about real events, twisting them a little, but still keeping them close to your heart is an important process.

Also, that way you can relive those events over and over again, and others will keep guessing what was the real part in it.

Strangely enough, it adds to its mystery (and excitement, of course)...

6. *What is your speciality and why?*

I would say it's mixing the past with the present. I'm not an expert, but I also love to keep up the suspense until the end. Although this doesn't always come through in my erotic stories, as they are linear, but in my paranormal romance books, I draw a parallel between what happened 500 years ago and what's happening right now. It's difficult to explain without revealing the plot itself, but I do love to play with the mind of the reader, if you know what I mean.

7. *Are there any topics you don`t like writing about?*

Now? Not really. If you asked me a few years ago, I would have said everything that involves sex ;)

I guess I just realized that I shouldn't say no, just because I don't know how something feels. If I don't try it, I will never know... If I'm not familiar with a topic, then

I do my research, but not too many things scare me nowadays (without wanting to sound weird or vain).

8. Do you have any tips / warnings for newbie erotica writers?

Follow your dreams. You will get some ugly feedback (or none at all), but that doesn't mean that your work isn't appreciated. Don't take them personally, but accept them, so that they can serve as stepping stones, helping you improve your writing. We all make mistakes; that's what makes us human.

Personally, I couldn't wait to grab a physical copy of my books, and that made up for whatever negativity I got (but luckily it has only been minor stuff so far).

So, if you are thinking about writing, or if you already have a story or two, try to make them into a book, no matter how tiny it is. Trust me, as soon as you have it on your shelf, you will become a different person.

9. What is your favourite season and why?

Spring, because that's when everything comes to life. I just love to watch the flowers blossom and the world wake up from its winter slumber. I always feel like I'm reborn myself every time springs comes (I know, I'm a hopeless romantic).